"HELLO READING books are a perfect introduction to reading. Brief sentences full of word repetition and full-color pictures stress visual clues to help a child take the first important steps toward reading. Mastering these story books will build children's reading confidence and give them the enthusiasm to stand on their own in the world of words."

—Bee Cullinan
Past President of the International Reading
Association, Professor in New York University's
Early Childhood and Elementary Education Program

"Readers aren't born, they're made. Desire is planted—planted by parents who work at it."

—Jim Trelease
author of *The Read Aloud Handbook*

"When I was a classroom reading teacher, I recognized the importance of good stories in making children understand that reading is more than just recognizing words. I saw that children who have ready access to story books get excited about reading. They also make noticeably greater gains in reading comprehension. The development of the HELLO READING stories grows out of this experience."

—Harriet Ziefert
M.A.T., New York University School of Education
Author, Language Arts Module,
Scholastic Early Childhood Program

PUFFIN BOOKS

Viking Penguin Inc., 40 West 23rd Street, New York, New York 10010, U.S.A.
Penguin Books Ltd, 27 Wrights Lane, London W8 5TZ (Publishing & Editorial) and
Harmondsworth, Middlesex, England (Distribution & Warehouse)
Penguin Books Australia Ltd., Ringwood, Victoria, Australia
Penguin Books Canada Limited, 2801 John St., Markham, Ontario, Canada L3R 1B4
Penguin Books (N.Z.) Ltd, 182–190 Wairau Road, Auckland 10, New Zealand

First published in Puffin Books, 1988 • Published simultaneously in Canada
Text copyright © Harriet Ziefert, 1988
Illustrations copyright © David Prebenna, 1988
All rights reserved • Printed in Singapore for Harriet Ziefert, Inc.

Library of Congress Cataloging-in-Publication Data
Ziefert, Harriet.
A clean house for mole and mouse.
(Hello reading! ; 12)
Summary: Mole and Mouse work hard cleaning and tidying their house and
spend the rest of the day outside so their house will stay clean.
[1. Moles (Animals)—Fiction.   2. Mice—Fiction.
3. House cleaning—Fiction]   I. Prebenna, David, ill.
II. Title.   III. Series: Ziefert, Harriet.   Hello reading! (Puffin Books) ; 12.
PZ7.Z487Ne   1988   [E]   87-25785
ISBN 0-14-050810-4

A Clean House for Mole and Mouse

Harriet Ziefert
Pictures by David Prebenna

PUFFIN BOOKS

"This is a nice house,"
said Mouse.
"But now it is dirty.
Let's clean it up."

"Okay," said Mole.
"Let's clean it up."

Mole and Mouse cleaned
the bedroom.

And the bedroom
looked just fine!

They cleaned the bathroom.

And the bathroom
looked just fine!

They cleaned the living room.

And the living room
looked just fine!

They cleaned the kitchen.

And the kitchen
looked just fine!

Mole said, "I'm tired
of making everything
so clean!"

"But we're almost done,"
said Mouse.

"If *you* wash the windows and *I* scrub the floor, then…

everything will be clean!"

"Now I'm hungry!"
said Mole.
"I want to cook."

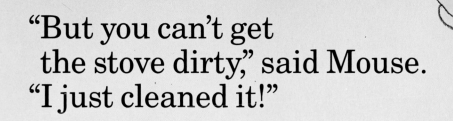

"But you can't get
  the stove dirty," said Mouse.
"I just cleaned it!"

"So I'll take a bath,"
said Mole.

"But you can't get
   the tub dirty," said Mouse.
"I just scrubbed it!"

"So I'll take a nap,"
said Mole.

"No! No!" yelled Mouse.
"I just made the bed!"

Mole asked, "What *can* I do if everything is so clean?"

"You can go outside,"
said Mouse.

"You can take a shower."

"You can take a nap."

"And then we can have
a fine picnic!"